The Berenstain Bears ®

Whoever you are,
wherever you're from,
you're welcome to Bear Country.
Glad you could come!

Mike Berenstain

Based on the characters created by
Stan and Jan Berenstain

HARPER FESTIVAL
An Imprint of HarperCollinsPublishers

HarperCollins
PUBLISHERS
Since 1817

Library of Congress Control Number: 2016936326   ISBN 978-0-06-235026-8
16 17 18 19 20 SCP 10 9 8 7 6 5 4 3 2 1 ❖ First Edition

A special guest was staying with the Bear family in their tree-house home down a sunny dirt road deep in Bear Country. It was their Cousin Tex, who lived on a ranch "way out west."

"It's the finest ranch you've ever seen," he said. "From the Rio Grande to Abilene!"

Cousin Tex had never been to Bear Country. He was eager to see all the sights.

"We'll ask Mayor Honeypot to show you around," said Papa.

"Good idea," agreed Mama. "The mayor knows everything there is to know about Bear Country."

So the family took Cousin Tex
down to the town hall.
    "Welcome to Bear Country!"
said Mr. Mayor, shaking Tex's hand.
    "Howdy!" said Tex.

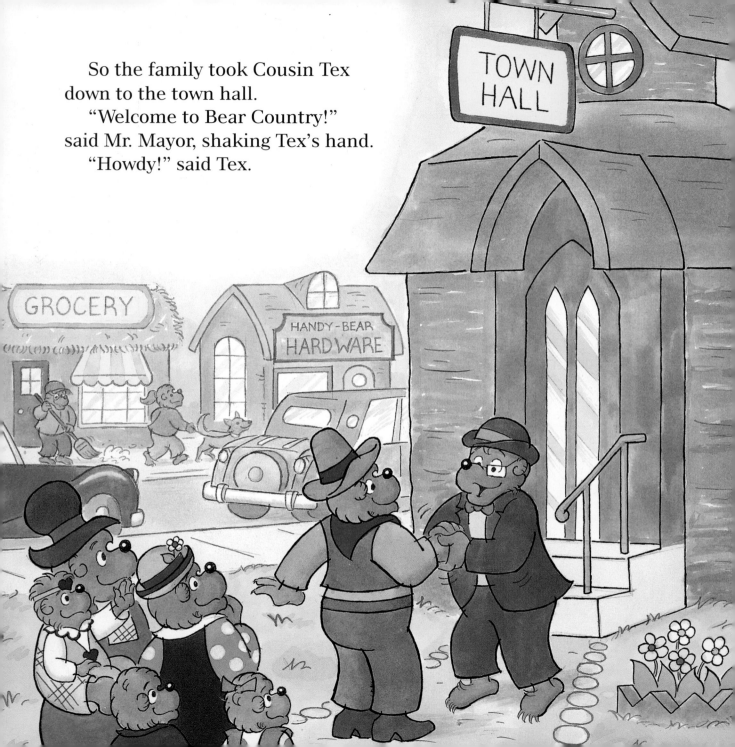

"Always glad to show a visitor around our fine community," said the mayor. "Hop into my long lavender limousine and we'll start right here in Bear Town."

"This is where Bear Country folks come to do their shopping and other things," said the mayor. "They go to the post office, stop by the library, and have a bite to eat, maybe stop by the clothing or flower shops. If there's anything you need, we've got it right here in Bear Town."

"What a commotion!" said Tex. "Back home we've just got the general store, a barbecue place, and the feed mill."

Leaving town, they stopped as a train pulled out of Bear Town Station.

"It looks a lot like the railway depot back home," said Cousin Tex.

"Meet Chief Bruno and Officer Marguerite," said the mayor. "They keep the peace and make sure everyone in Bear Country is safe and secure."

"Howdy!" said Tex. "Always glad to meet the local peace officers. Back home Marshal Bruin keeps an eye on things."

Just outside town, they stopped at the Bearsonian Institution. Professor Actual Factual showed them around.

"We have many exhibits," said the professor. "Dinosaur fossils, historic aircraft, precious gems, and the Gallery of Great Bear Art."

"Golly!" said Tex. "There's not much like this back home—just the Western History Museum."

"What's on exhibit there?" asked the professor.

"They have the disguise that Billy the Cub wore while robbing the bank at Fort Grizzly."

"Golly!" said the professor, impressed.

"Here's another impressive Bear Country sight," said the mayor as they drove on. "Squire Grizzly's mansion."

"My stars!" said Tex. "Quite a sizable spread."

Squire and Lady Grizzly greeted them and showed them into a hall hung with paintings.

"These are portraits of my ancestors," said Squire Grizzly proudly.

"Land sakes!" said Tex. "This feller here looks like my Great Uncle Zeke, who wrastled a mountain lion and tied its tail into a necktie."

"My stars!" said Lady Grizzly.

"In the valley just beyond Grizzly Hall," said Mayor Honeypot, "we find a classic scene of Bear Country peace and plenty—the rolling hills and fields of Farmer Ben's farm."

"And there's our tree house just beyond!" said Sister, pointing.

"It certainly is a pretty picture," said Tex. "Reminds me of my own ranch land back home. We have a few more cows, of course."

"In the next valley," Mayor Honeypot went on, "we find a very different picture."

They drove into deep, dark woods.

"Why, this is Great Spooky Forest," said Papa.

"That's right," said the mayor. "The home of . . ."

"THE SPOOKY OLD TREE!" they all said, shivering.

"Another spooky Bear Country spot is Giant Bat Cave," said Mayor Honeypot, parking at the cave entrance.

He lit a torch and led them in. Huge rock formations loomed up.

"These are stalactites and stalagmites," said the mayor.

"Which are which?" asked Brother.

"'Tites are on the top; 'mites are on the bottom," explained the mayor.

Suddenly, a cloud of bats flew out.
"Yeow!" cried Papa, heading for the exit. He didn't care for bats.
"This makes me think of the old cliff dwellings back home," said Cousin Tex. "Plenty of bats there—mighty big ones!"

"Truth to tell," said Cousin Tex, "I have!"

"I've saved the most truly spectacular thing in all Bear Country for last," said the mayor. "Our national treasure—the Old Honey Tree!"

They gazed at the thick, twisty old tree. Bees buzzed around. The smell of honey was in the air. Sweet, golden, sticky honey oozed from the trunk.

"YUM!" said all the bears.

Cousin Tex stuck out his tongue to catch a drip. But the bees buzzed out in an angry cloud. The bears jumped into Mayor Honeypot's limousine and sped away.

Luckily the mayor's limousine was faster than the bees. They made it back to Bear Town mostly unstung.

"Cousin Tex," said Mayor Honeypot, "I'd like to present you with a sample of our most precious possession—Bear Country's golden honey."

"Mmm-mmm!" said Cousin Tex, taking a taste. "There's nothing back home that can hold a candle to this. But you know . . . ," he added, "be it ever so humble, there's no place like home."

"How true!" said the mayor. "And you are very welcome in our home anytime."

"Yes," his cousins told him. "Welcome to Bear Country!"

"Thank you kindly!" said Cousin Tex.